An Imprint of HarperCollinsPublishers

When I see my reflection...

...I guess that's me.

You two ready?

COMING!

flick

3

It's a zoo in here today. Let's move quickly.

Lorelai, did you bring the list?

Yep!

It says, "You must have **five distinct** highlighters for literature class!"

Intense, right?

I'll shop for new art supplies any day!

Do you need any fun stuff for your locker, Jay?

Nah, I'm good.

Got everything?

Yep! Think we could go clothes shopping sometime soon, though?

I'd like some cute stuff to go out in.

Sure, dear. Any cute boys in your class?

Maybe!

Don't touch your face, sweetheart.

I'm not!

Remember, Mom will pick you up from school, not the transfer station.

Okay.

SLIDE

Jay! Over here!

Brace!

How was your summer?

Radio silence, man!

Sorry about that. Family time, y'know?

BUT! Wait 'til you hear my latest additions!

Ooh, gimme!

GUESS WHAT?!

What?

13

7:45 A.M.
Ybor City,
Downtown Tampa

WASHINGTON
MIDDLE MAGNET
International Studies
WELCOME

You're not coming to the courtyard?

I have to get my schedule fixed.

I'll catch up later.

Jay Violet.

15

...I'm sorry, Jay. We won't be able to do that.

What?!

Why?

Why can't I take art this year?

How about band?

Yes, Jay?

I think I left my folder of sheet music yesterday.

Yes, you did.

So I threw it away.

My serious students don't forget their folders.

Ugh, NO.

Orchestra, then!

DO I SEE A PIZZA PIE HAND?

Uh...

That's it. Tape this tack under your violin arm.

NO.

Uh, what about...

NO.

Art class.

You said we take a wheel of electives in sixth and seventh grade so that in eighth we can pick what we **want**.

Everyone else got their choice.

SIGH

Most honors track students don't pick art, so it doesn't fit easily in your block schedule.

Let's see...

Hm.

I think the only way to do this is if you are a TA during third period, with lunch one and P.E.—

YES!

I'll do it!

I'll need special approval if I do this for you...

!

!!!

All right.

You'll have art with Mr. Dunlap.

ADMINISTRATION

Whew.

That was scary.

But now this year will be perfect.

Good morning, everyone.

I know you want to catch up. You may talk quietly while I take roll.

You? Almost tardy on the first day? I never thought I'd see that!

Psht!

Johnny got a bass. This band is gonna happen!

Awesome!

Did you get your schedule fixed?

We're in lunch two.

Lemme check.

Oh, I'm Lunch one.

Psst—Claire!

Hey, Jay! How was your summer?

Good, yours?

Over too soon, y'know?

What lunch are you in this year?

Two! How about you?

I'm in one. How about Edie?

Two as well, I think.

This sucks!

Maybe my friends are running late...

Uh, may I sit here?

Fine.

...or not.

Guess I'll bring a book tomorrow.

GYMNASIUM

FIGHTING
HORNE[T]

Let's go, five
laps around!

RIIIII NNNGG

YAWN

Jay, man, I haven't
seen you all day!

I know!
It's weird.

Aren't you
taking the bus?

My mom's
picking me
up today.

Cool.
See ya
tomorrow.

Jay, over here!

How was school?

Fine, I guess.

You know, I can take the bus like last year, so you don't have to drive all the way out here.

Then you wouldn't get home until almost 4:30, sitting at the transfer for so long. Such a waste of time.

Lorelai **hates** losing all that time with all her IB homework, and her school is only fifteen minutes from here.

Well, if I had to take the bus, I wouldn't mind.

24

Later...

What're you doing?

NOTHING!

Mm-hmm...

chew
chew

You know you can always use my CleariGel. It's right here. Or my—

NO.

I'm fine, I don't need it.

CHOP!

HEY!

That stuff doesn't work anyway.

Not to mention what happened last year.

Back when I still had lunch with my friends.

Edie, what's that?

CleariGel. It's for zits.

We can't all have perfect skin like you, Jay.

Oh, I thought that stuff was brown. At least the kind I use is...

27

But it popped back up again during P.E. thanks to that jerk Aaron.

Psst, hey!

Hey, Jay!

Haha...You were right, Edie.

Jay IS wearing makeup!

HA HA
HA HA
HA
HA

And Aaron wouldn't drop it.

Better hustle, **pretty boy!**

Look at those rosy cheeks. Jay wearing all that makeup.

I wanted to call him a goblin-face.

HEY, JAY!

WHAT, Aaron?

But that would have been too mean.

31

You're both here! Wonderful!

I'm so excited.

I've never had teaching assistants before.

I'll have to get you access to the copy room.

I'm sure you'll both recognize some of these assignments.

You'll separate them for my sixth and seventh graders.

We put the worksheets in folders, right?

Ah, the folders! I left them in the teachers' lounge.

I'll be right back!

And they're not worksheets, they're enrichment activities!

Glad I'm not alone in here.

eyeroll

Lunch, on the other hand...

There's gotta be someone I can sit with **today**.

Let's see...

All girls' table?

Can't do that.

Popular jerk boys' table?

Desperate times...

GULP

...call for desperate measures!

Hi, Ryan, Gene...

Mind if I sit?

Sure, man, whatever.
Gene was saying that he made out with three girls this summer.

But I don't believe him.

You weren't there!

33

Bet your parents were though!

Shut up!

Heh...

Well, well, Porcelain Doll, we meet again.

Hi, Aaron.

Your mommy pack you a nice little lunch, buuuuddy?

I, uh...

Nah, it's cool. Sit with us.

HAHA HA HAHA

HA HA HA HA HA

HEY! There are other people in this courtyard, y'know!

Y'all need to hush up!

Oooh, well excuse me, maybe if you didn't have such a funny face!

WHAT DID YOU SAY?!

Whoa! Don't get so close. I'd hate to fall into **that** GAP.

HA

WHAT?!

Haha, **dude!**

Aaron's freakin' hilarious!

SLAP

Haha, yeah...

What're YOU laughing at, RUDOLPH?

Shouldn't you be off guiding Santa's sleigh?

RUDOLPH!

HAHAHA

35

Many of you know the drill. For the first class we'll begin by making portfolios to keep our projects safe.

Please work quietly for the next twenty minutes.

Wish I had art class every day.

This is more like it.

...

What is she looking at?!

HUNCH

Wait...Isn't Mark in this class?

Oh.

Maybe he doesn't think we're friends.

Psst, hey, I'm Amy.

I'm Jay.

Are you new?

Yeah, I went to Adams last year.

Quiet, please. We'll be moving on shortly.

GULP.

Cool fortune teller lady, by the way.

Don't look!

At home

Have you tried my Strike Out wipes? I don't care if you use them.

I already tried them, but nothing happened.

URGH. It's just so annoying! I didn't have acne last year!

Hey, what are you two arguing about? The table needs to be set for dinner.

We aren't fighting. Jay's skin keeps breaking out.

Have you tried lying out in the sun yet?

Yes, Dad. I just get all sweaty. I think that makes it **worse**.

It's **fine**. Let's stop talking about it!

SIGH

It's not fair.

I didn't even do anything!

They don't understand.

Why me?

I don't understand. None of you have bad skin!!

I had plenty of breakouts as a kid.

It doesn't look like it! I don't want my face to be all scarred.

Lots of kids have acne.

Maybe you should go see a dermatologist?

...

I'll make an appointment.

G'morning, Brace.

Hey.

Hmm...

Good choice.

BRACE!

What's up, Casey?

Check it out! I got the latest Amp Hero catalog!

Coming!

Sorry about earlier.

No worries. I mean...

Ms. Fulton **does** like her worksheets!

HA. True!

Think she'll ever let us use the copier again?

Jay, who're you talking to?

Oh!

No one, I guess...

You're reading *Misfortune's Orphans*, too?! That series is *SO* good.

I'm obsessed. Have you read book five?

You have book five?! Can I borrow it sometime?

Sure!

Quiet, please. There should be no talking during our warm-up.

Yes, Mr. Dunlap.

BEAUTY ✦ MAVEN ✦

The years will pass but you will be ageless.

INQUIRE TODAY

Soon I'll be beautiful, too...

CHECK-IN

Airbrushed and poreless!

Haha, probably not.

I'll try anything, though.

Whatever it takes.

Everyone here already has nice skin ... or they're old.

I hate that it's obvious why I'm here.

They're all just vain. I have an actual problem!

Jay Violet?

UGH, now everyone knows my name!

Hang tight and Dr. North will be right in.

She has acne scars.

She gets it.

...Think we're all good with your forms.

So, I hear we're having some acne trouble.

Whoa. He looks like a Ken doll.

His skin looks fake. He's an alien.

Bet you'd love for **that** to go away.

Um...yes.

Well, we have to start somewhere. Let's begin with a bit of minocycline.

That might be all you need. And be sure to wash your face before bed with this sulfur wash.

Come back and see me in two weeks and we'll see how you're progressing.

That's it?

All right.

Here goes nothin'.

Yuck. This smells awful.

splash

RATTLE

GLUG GLUG

Gulp

Two weeks.

Two weeks and it's gone.

I can handle that.

47

I don't want to be too extreme too quickly. There's always **Accutane**, but let's see if this does the trick.

Oh, ya know, there are also some topicals we can try out. Hang tight a minute.

How's **this** for a goody bag? This'll keep you stocked for awhile.

Whoa, there's a lot in here.

I wrote out a list for what to use and when.

And here's your new prescription.

Good grief.

Hi, Jay!

How's my ol' pal Rudolph this fine morning?

Snicker

Buzz off, Aaron!

Aw, I thought we were friends.

HA HA

What are we? Fifth graders?

That's just Aaron being his normal, annoying self.

KICK ME

Once you get the stations set up for map making, feel free to take a study period.

Back in a bit!

Colored Pencils

PLONK

Hey, Mark?

How come you don't sit with me in art?

I don't know. I didn't think you wanted me to.

I'm not in with the cool kids like you.

What?! No I'm not!

Okay, sure.

"In with the cool kids?!"

Psht, no way!

I'm not mean like them...

S'il vous plait, regardez ça.

...am I?

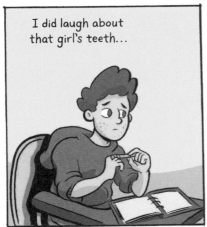

I did laugh about that girl's teeth...

No.

They tease me, too!

They all have perfect skin or clothes and talk about girls and sports nonstop.

We're not the same.

We don't even look like we'd be friends.

HEY!

I am NOT one of the cool kids!

No one even sits with me at lunch!

Aren't you friends with like Brace, Casey, Aaron, Edie...

Brace, yeah, but I'm not really close with the others.

Hmm.

Sigh, this isn't working either.

Time to kick things into high gear!

May I use the computer for a bit?

Yeah, one sec.

SEARCH

What is accutane?

INQUIRE   RANDOM

Skin peels off like an alien.

It's intense.

SKIN BLOG

Super dried out!

Awful, but it worked.

Buy good lip balm.

Changes in mood.

Isotretinoin.

Clear now.

Worth the trouble.

Only thing that worked for me.

Boys have it easier.

Long-term side effects?

My Experie

Hey, Dad?

Do you think we could go to that other dermatologist?

I think I want to try Accutane and—

The one Mom's friend recommended?

Yeah.

Okay!

THANK YOU!

All right. Get the number and let's call.

Hmm.

SWIPE

I have a good feeling about this!

What did Mom's friend say about Dr. Laski?

That he was "odd but really good."

BAY SKIN CLINIC

Jay?

Yes.

Let's take a look.

Hmm.

Okay.

Okay.

Dr. North had you try minocycline and doxycycline?

Yes.

The culture he took shows your acne is resistant to both of those.

Really?

And you used all these topicals?

Yes.

Notice any improvements?

Not really.

If some of these were helping, I'd consider a new configuration.

But they aren't.

I'd like to try to knock this out with isotretinoin.

Accutane?

Yes, that's one of the brand names.

It'll be intense. There are lots of hoops to jump through. But I think it's our best bet at getting you clear once and for all.

That's what I read online... Do we start with a low dose?

No. I'm putting you on the highest dose. I want you to do one full six-month cycle and be done with it.

There's monthly blood work to check your triglyceride levels. If they get too high, you'll have to adjust your diet.

Okay.

If we have to stop mid-cycle, the whole treatment is less effective and your acne will return.

I understand.

BY CLICKING ACCEPT, YOU ACKNOWLEDGE THAT YOU'VE READ AND UNDERSTOOD THE ABOVE.

ACCEPT.

CLICK

DIAGNOSTIX LABS

Almost done.

PICK UP

DROP OFF

RX

Go grab the things Dr. Laski recommended.

Here we go!

Chapped Lips Stix

Vaselips

Petroleum Jelly

Please work.

face moisturizer

face wash

vaseline lip balm

ISOTRETINOIN

Take your morning pill?

Yep!

Bye, Mom.

TRANSFER!

Oof, the humidity today.

PLONK
Slide

Too hot.

It's not even that sunny out.

Goodbye, hoodie.

Definitely don't need you today!

SHAKE
SHAKE

It's not that hard... Just ask.

Mark... want to sit with me and Amy in art today?

Okay, sure.

I'll see if Alisha from my table wants to join us.

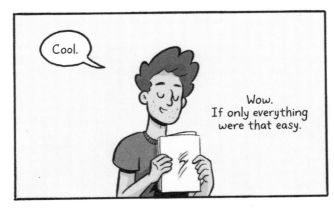

Cool.

Wow. If only everything were that easy.

Attention, artists!

Any guesses what project we're starting today?

Portraits, self-portraits, and still lifes!

Let's warm up with some quick doodles of everyone at your table, yourself included.

Scribble
Scribble

Love how you drew my hair, Alisha. It looks like noodles.

Whoa. These are like real portraits. How do you draw so fast?

I dunno...

Dang, Mark.

Whoa. No fair.

But look, we both drew Jay wrong.

Huh? Whaddya mean?

Don't say my skin.

We both drew him with his hoodie on.

And he's not even wearing it.

I don't ALWAYS wear a hoodie.

Yes, you do.

But it's so hot out!

That's never stopped you before.

Can't believe they noticed that...

Okay, everyone stop looking at me!

Beep Beep

Beep Beep

5:00 AM

Beep Beep

Ugh.

WHAP!

Beep Click

5:00 AM

flick

These early mornings are—

Oh, no!

IT'S GOTTEN WORSE?!

Umm...

I–I don't know. I wasn't paying attention.

I know, Mr. Harold!

Yes, Kristen?

Losing your touch, smarty-pants?

Why is everything— everyone—so annoying today?

And this heat, too.

I'm suffo—

BUMP

Oh, I didn't realize it was you, Jay. Need a hand?

No, I'm fine.

How's your week going?

Super weird.

I felt really grumpy yesterday. But today I feel fine.

That's probably because you're in art class.

Always makes me feel better.

Yeah, same.

I guess!

I don't know.

Dr. Laski said irritability was a side effect...

I feel...

...all foggy.

We'll be in the café.

Okay.

Fantasy / Sci

Art & How-To

Figure Drawing

CARTOON ANIMALS

ANATOMY

TEXTURE

LANDSCAPES

♪

NEW

Hm.

STYLED Guy

No. 129

4 Simple

Look your BEST

No matter what you look like!

MAGAZINE

MEN'S INTEREST

Forget "fashion." Style is all about how you make yourself look and feel your best. All you need are a few staples and the proper fit for your body. Learn by example:

I wonder...

Hey.

We're just about ready. Will you find Lorelai?

Sure.

Can I page her from customer service?

NO.

Boo, no fun!

Have you paid for that book, ma'am?

Funny.

Ready to go?

Yep.

TRAVEL

Are you and Mom still going clothes shopping tomorrow?

Yeah, why?

Do you want to come with us?

Sure, I'll tag along ... why not?

75

I found a few things.

Whoa, okay.

I like this color.

It's nice, right?

Is this okay? A few of them are on clearance...

Yes, I think it's fine...

It's your birthday soon anyway. May I wrap a few of them?

Yeah!

Are you sure about these sizes? Don't you want them roomier?

Nope. They're **exactly** right. I tried all of them on already and everything.

If you say so...

Are you cleaning out your closet?!!

It's an anomaly.

If there are things to donate, put them in the kitchen.

I will.

I didn't know dressing up could make me feel like this!

Should I gel my hair, too?!

My stupid face.

URGH.

Stop. Don't think about it.

Hair.

GEL

POMADE

Hmm. Maybe.

I'll try this for a bit.

We're up at the crack of dawn to go get your blood drawn before school... and you're smiling?

Who are you and what have you done with my son?

Haha. I don't know. I just like my new outfit.

Dressing up for anything, or **anyone**, in particular?

Moooom.

Okay okay, I'm only asking.

I'm doing it for **myself** because I want to.

I'm doing this...for myself...

... because...

Wipe

... I want to.

Gulp

And we're all set. Your doctor will have the results in two days.

Thank you.

Jay!

Cute shirt! Is it new?

Thanks, Claire. It is.

Ah, yes.

My plan is working!

Muahaha!

Great look, Jay!

Thanks, Edie.

You're all dressed up today... Is it picture day or something?

No... I'm not **that** dressed up. It's just a new shirt.

Jay!

This is great! No one's looking at my face!

Well, well, well, aren't we looking **fancy** today.

I guess...

Just look at this hair. Who're you trying to impress?

No one, Aaron.

Then you won't care if I rough it up a bit?

HEY!

Stop it!

HA HA HA

83

Mm-hmm. Mm-hmm.

It's so dry.

My face feels crinkly.

Yes, that's how it works, pushing it to the surface and drying it all out.

Chapped lips? Overheating? Changes in mood?

I get kinda warm and sweaty randomly.

And sometimes I can peel entire layers off my lips!

Wear light layers and keep using the Vaseline and you'll be fine.

As for your blood work... your triglyceride levels are looking pretty high and we want to avoid long-term liver damage.

I want you on a low-fat diet. Really consider what you're eating and we'll check the labs again next month.

This is more of a precaution. No need to worry.

Take your pills—don't miss a dose.
Wash your face—but don't overdo it.

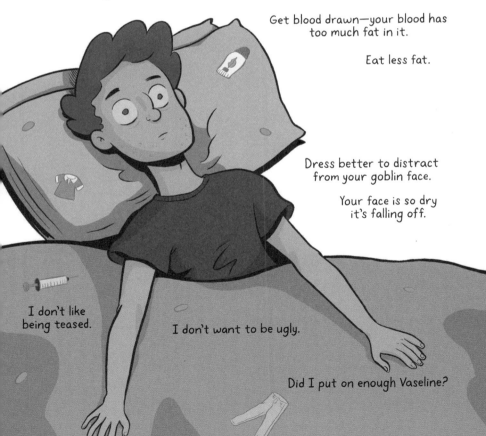

Get blood drawn—your blood has too much fat in it.

Eat less fat.

Dress better to distract from your goblin face.

Your face is so dry it's falling off.

I don't like being teased.

I don't want to be ugly.

Did I put on enough Vaseline?

Almost out of hair gel.

Wait! I have this other stuff from my last haircut.

Pomade. Is this like gel?

"Stays wet for all-day restyling."

STAY SLICK MOLDABLE POMADE

Ms. Carvey, homework?

Yes.

Mr. Violet?

Yes.

Mr. Redding, homework?

Yeah.

Ah...

Heyyy, Buuuuddy.

...our specimen approaches.

Its curiosity builds.

It can't hold back.

Heyyy...

Buuud—

SPLAT

Gotcha.

UGH, GROSS!

What did you put in your hair?

Huh? What do you mean?

Mr. Thompson! I need the bathroom pass!

Jay put something weird in his hair.

Well, Mr. Redding, maybe in the future you'll keep your hands off Mr. Violet.

You can wait until after class. My lesson begins now.

HA

HA HA

That's enough.

Settle down, everyone.

giggle

Eyes forward.

Nice.

I think I'm a pomade guy.

Finally.

I want to get this done before it gets too hot out.

Did you bring the trash bags?

Yep.

YAWN

Start bagging up everything, then you can help me cut it back.

I'll hold, you bag.

Fine.

PUSH

Oof!

Ew, don't get it on me!

I thought you liked this vine?

Thunbergia. I love it. But I'm worried about the weight of it on the fence. It's just a haircut, we're not killing it.

Thank you both for your help.

I can't believe there's any left.

I have homework. I'm going inside.

...

MOM, DAD!

UGH, it's so hot.

Hey, Claire, Edie.

Ooh, Jay, we're doing a survey while we wait.

Oh?

First, pick your favorite: Ms. Corbin or Ms. Fulton?

I guess Ms. Fulton if I have to pick.

Mr. Richards or Ms. Sparrow?

Ugh, neither!

You gotta pick one!

Fine. Ms. Sparrow.

Kate Winslet or Kate Beckinsale?

I don't know... This is dumb, they're both pretty.

You have to CHOOSE!

Kate Winslet? ... I don't know!

RIIIINGG

Jay.

Helloooo

EARTH TO JAY!

AH! What?!

Phone for you.

Thanks.

It's a *girl*.

OKAY THANK YOU GOODBYE.

H-hello?

Oh, hi!

Hey, Mom?

May I go to the movies tonight?

CITRUS MALL

I'll pick you up at nine thirty.

Thanks, Mom.

Hey, Amy!

Thanks for meeting me. Sorry I was being weird earlier.

It's all good. You live closer than most people, so it was easy to convince my parents.

Blech, parents.

Right, sorry, we can talk about whatever.

We still haven't picked a movie.

Oooh ... I do wanna see *Mysterious Mr. Music*, but...

That was pretty good. I liked it.

I did, too.

I never come to the mall on a weeknight. This is fun.

Thanks for meeting me.

My mom and dad were bugging me.

They're getting a divorce, I think.

It's nice to get a break from them.

Secretly, I dream about sneaking away and living on my own! Just like *Misfortune's Orphans!*

Whoa, really?

What? Don't YOU have any secrets?

NO!

Just a perfect angel.

Yeah, right! I hate when people call me "perfect."

What'd you expect?

You get good grades.

You're nice to everyone.

It's not a bad thing.

Then how come it doesn't sound like a compliment?

SHRUG

So, your brother goes to King High? I wonder if he knows my sister, Lorelai.

Small world. Maybe.

Hey.

Yeah?

Is that lady waving at us your mom?

WHAT?

Oh my god! She's so embarrassing.

Thanks again, Jay, for meeting me...I'm glad we're friends.

Yeah, me too, Amy. See ya.

Chew Chew

9:47
CHARGED

Hi, Ms. Flowers, it's Jay Violet.

Is Brace there?

Hi, Jay. He stayed over at Riley's tonight.

Do you have his number?

That's all right. I'll just talk to him at school tomorrow.

Thank you. G'night.

Hi, Sweetums.

mrow

Tap
Tap

Go away.

Hi.

What do you want?

STRETCH

Are you all right?

No.

I'm annoyed.

Pat Pat

Literally school has taken over. I don't have time for anything else. Maybe IB is good for getting into college, but I want more.

Would you drop out?

I've been thinking about it.

Whoa, really?

I have to talk to Mom and Dad, though.

DINNER!

We can play HORSE after if you want.

You're on.

But no mercy.

It's not what I wanted to see. Your triglycerides are elevated. No cause for concern, though.

It's only month three. You really need to be diligent about your diet.

I don't want to stop the cycle, but if we can't get these down, I'll **have** to.

And I'd hate to impede the progress I'm seeing.

Let's knock this out!

Oof. I'm tired.

Probably the heat.

Ms. F didn't leave us that much to do today...

What're you doing?

SHRUG

Drawing.

Good idea!

And I thought I drew a lot.

POP

It's like a **bonus** art class!

No wonder Mark is so good.

MROW

No, no, kitty. Off the table.

Someone's got a birthday coming up.

Oooh, are you gonna have a party?!

It's so close to winter break and the holidays. I don't think anyone will come.

And we live kinda out of the way...

What? Of course they will. You haven't even asked anyone yet.

I'll think about it.

Next Saturday would be okay with us, sweetheart.

You can draw a cute invitation!

Will anyone come?

Aren't birthday parties for babies?

It would be fun to have my friends over...

I can dress up... That will help.

Couple of legs...

and a little face here...

Perfect.

Bye, Dad.

See you tonight.

And let me know what you think of your lunch!

I will. Byyyye.

Brace and I used to brainstorm band names together...

Last year.

I would've drawn it for the band.

Psst, Claire, I'm having a party. Will you give one to Edie next period?

Fun! Yeah, no problem.

Mark, I'm having a party next weekend.

Cool. I'll ask my mom if she'll drive me.

What d'ya say, Kristen?

Hehe. I love the cake's little feet!

Thanks! Casey?

Yes, dude, let's party it up!

Casey's more Brace's friend than mine, but that's cool he wants to come!

And one final invite...

Psst.

Cute shirt!

Thanks.

You didn't have to get all dressed up for my party.

Uh, I'm actually going out tonight. Figured you'd want the time alone with your friends.

Oh yeah, that's cool. Not like you won't be home on my real birthday anyway.

True!

But you still better save me some cake!

I make no promises. That's the risk you take by not attending.

Don't EVEN!

Hmm, it's not so bad today...

Right?

Someone's here!

It's nine thirty, you can't sleep away the entire break!

I'm not!

The days of winter break slowly blurred together.

I tried my best to conquer them...

...so they wouldn't slip away.

...For the most part.

Hi, Ms. Flowers, it's Jay.

Just like old times.

BZt!

DING DONG

131

You're here!

I'm glad you called.

Sorry I missed your party. My dad surprised Alice and me and took us out to dinner.

No worries!

Hi, Jay.

You too.

Hi, Ms. Flowers. Nice to see you.

I like all your Christmas decorations.

Oh, thank you.

Although I guess it's time to take them down.

It's nice to enjoy them.

My mom takes them down Christmas night.

Mom said if I cleaned up the garage we could practice here.

It's been great.

FFp!

We're mostly learning covers right now, but Casey and Riley have written some songs.

That's awesome.

Are you gonna have a show?

I want to hear you all play!

Heh. Funny you should say that.

Squeak

The guys will be here soon...

Today's one of the few days of break we could all meet.

Hope that's okay? You get a free concert!

Oh.

Yeah, of course.

That's cool.

PINK RHIN

Wait... are they all hanging out...

...without me?

1-2-3!

PINK RHINOS

Wow.

So what do you think then? Six?

Yeah, and if three are original, that'd be amazing. Everyone will expect a few covers.

Let's coordinate our looks, too. Black button-up, jeans, something pink, like a tie, a hat, or laces.

Yeah, I'm down!

There's that kiosk at the mall with funky accessories. Near where we saw Jay that time.

Wait, when was this?

You were with that new girl, Amy. Oooooh!

We have Spanish together. She's pretty cute.

Eh, eh? What's going on there?

Nothing, we're just friends.

"Friends," oooooh.

I'm not lying!

Jay's not like Carter. I thought you and Heather were in love, but now there's Sara.

Heh.

Casey here thinks he's got Megan under his spell.

Whatever! You're not in math with us to see.

Mm-hmmm!

I may not have a six-pack like Will here,

but wait 'til she sees this!

Dude!!

Nice.

Mine's way smoother—step back.

By all means, Your Majesty.

Jay, you can borrow mine.

Okay, sure.

139

Uhhh, what do I do?

WHOA!

Don't fall.

DON'T FALL.

Jay, you okay?

HA HA HA

OOF!

Yeah, I'm good.

The wipeout gets us all, dude.

Heh, yeah.

Think I'll stay grounded. Don't wanna hurt my drawing hand.

You didn't have to go if you were scared of getting hurt!

No, I—

It's fine. I can watch you all.

Since when does Brace skateboard anyway?

Since when did everything...

change?

And that's all I need. We'll see you next month.

Great, thanks.

YOUR HEALTH MATTERS

What was that look?

Nothing.

The needle... the blood draw... You didn't even flinch.

Mm-hmm.

Mm-hmm.

Your triglyceride levels have lowered. I'm pleased to see that.

We'll still keep an eye on them. Whatever food changes you've implemented are working.

You also have very few new breakouts. And all of it appears to be flattening.

Things are looking up.

Psst. Hi, Jay. Happy new year.

You go to Washington, don't you?

Mm-hmm Yeah, why?

Do you know Bart Flowers and Riley Morris?

You mean Brace? Yeah, I know him.

The Pink Rhinos?!

Yeah, that's their band.

Wow, that's so cool!!

Is it?

What? It's hot.

The AC is on.

So? I'm still hot!

SHAKE SHAKE SHAKE

Didn't you just put that on?

My lips are chapped! What else am I supposed to do?

I just never noticed how often you put it on until now.

tap tap   tap

Sorry I couldn't come to your birthday. My mom said it was too far from Apollo Beach.

No, I get it, it's okay.

I made you a card...but I lost the invite, so I didn't have your address.

You DREW it?!

Of course.

People never draw ME cards.

Thanks, Mark. This really made my day.

Hey, Amy.

Hi!

Brrr.

Mr. Dunlap always has it **freezing** in here.

I guess. It feels fine to me.

Maybe you should bring your new hoodie in case you need it.

I left it in my locker...
It's too warm out for me today.

Remember your biweekly creative book report is due next week.

You may choose any of the twenty options, but you may only use each option once.

Mr. Harold?

Yes, Casey?

Most of these options involve art and writing, but what about music?

Music is creative and involves writing, and that's my area of expertise, as you know.

So long as it's a solo effort outside of the Rhinos, Casey, I'm open to new ideas. That goes for any of you.

I'm excited to see your creativity shine through with these reports.

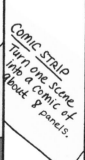

COMIC STRIP
Turn one scene into a comic of about 8 panels.

What about your other schoolwork?

I'm getting it all finished. This is homework, too.

All right...

Hi, Jay.

Hey, Riley.

Yeah, man. Friday works for me.

Sweet. Brace, Casey, and Will are down, too. Just some chill hang time.

KUH CHUK

Can your mom give me a ride to the mall?

Yep. I got you.

No music, no skateboarding? Count me in.

Asseyez-vous, Monsieur Violet.

Pardon, Madame Ehrlich.

Psst, Casey.

Yo.

I was thinking of maybe going to the mall on Friday. Wanna hang?

Eh, not sure I can. Rhinos practice.

Oh, right...

Hmm.

I'll talk to Brace.

RIIING

Brace!

Where are you headed?

I've got TA hour since I have art later. You?

English.

Feel like going to the mall or something on Friday?

Oh, um...I might have some family stuff.

Thought you might just be hanging out with the Rhinos again...

...well, yeah, kinda.

And I can't come? Why not? I hung out with you all before.

You're not really part of the group...

Carter and Will aren't even in the band!

They're different. They're **cool**.

You and I hung out all **the time** last year.

That was **different**.

You just want to draw or watch movies. It's **boring**. We like to go skating, talk about girls and music, and **jam** together.

Why don't you hang out with that weirdo, Mark, who never talks to anyone?

That's not true, he talks a lot. Just maybe not to jerks like you who think being in a band makes you **better** than everyone.

Whatever, Jay!

Stop trying to fit in where you **don't** belong.

Forget to put your **makeup** on today?

I'll never be cool.

Not with a face like **this**.

tap

Haha. Dropped your **lipstick**, freak!

SHUT UP, AARON!

RIIIIIIING

Heya!

Thought maybe you were absent today.

Is this stack for us?

Yup!

Is everything all right?

SHRUG

TAP TAP

Jay?

May I ask you something?

Hm?

No, no, that's okay! I wasn't sure.

If I'm being honest...

I don't really feel that way about **anyone.**

I think there might be some piece of me that's missing.

I don't think that's true.

Only **you** know what you feel inside.

You don't have to like anyone.

Thanks, Mark.

You really like me?

Ha, well, yeah. You're easy to talk to and we like similar stuff...

You're one of my only friends at this whole school.

I can't believe someone likes me...

Pimples and all?

...We used to hang out all the time.

But now it's like he doesn't think I fit in with him.

I'm sorry, Jay.

Maybe it's good that he and I only have one class together, after all.

Looks like Amy's working with Alisha today. Want to sit together?

Sure.

Are y'all fighting, too?

I'm still figuring that out.

What class do you and Brace have together?

Science.

I wish I could turn my brain off for a bit...

Next period.

...and not think about this.

But I don't think that's possible.

Aren't you nervous?

About what, Casey?

The **test**, dude! The morning class got theirs back.

Oh, right. I forgot.

Kristen and Brace—

Perfect as always.

COMPETITIVE VIBES

Jay and Casey...

flip

Not your best work.

EXAM 2   Jay V.

D+

what happened?

Ah! My parents are gonna kill me!

Mine too. Today sucks.

Excellent, Simon.

Impassioned as always, Kristen.

Pretty epic, Katie.

Very impressive, Jay.

Thank you.

Mr. Harold, you said I could play mine, right?!

Let's go with your favorite for now and see if we have more time at the end of class.

This one's called "Beowulf's Heart Thumps"!

Ooooh
wow
So cool

You really ran with this wonderful comic, Jay. A+

JAY VIOLET

HMPH

166

Greetings, artists. Today we venture into all-new territory!

There's **excitement!**

There's **danger!**

There's potential domestic practicality!

Today we travel to a new **DIMENSION!**

Today we're making...

ROBOTS!!

WHOA! COOL!

Part one begins with your designs, but they shouldn't just **look** interesting...

You must be able to construct them in 3D using cardboard, paper, and other useful objects.

Make sure you consider **all sides** of your robot.

Is it symmetrical?

Different colors?

Shapes?

Finally, we can draw however we want.

I want mine to be like a 3D cartoon.

Looking good, everyone.

Cool shapes on yours, Amy.

Thanks.

Hey, Mr. Dunlap?

On the back of mine, I want it to have a clock key, like he winds up.

What about a pencil?

Cut the key out of paper, glue it to a pencil and put it through a hole in the back.

You could cut it out of paper or use a pipe cleaner...

But I want it to actually turn.

Hm, I'll think on it.

What a great idea!

Thanks, Amy!

Sure.

So then we know radium has...

Seven energy levels or electron shells.

Because?

It falls on the seventh period, or row. And it has eighty-eight protons.

That's right!

See? You're both ready for next week's test. Sometimes it really is about saying it out loud to commit it to memory.

Seriously, you two have **nothing** to worry about for this test.

Okay...

Jay! Your mom will be here in ten minutes.

Thanks, Mrs. Singleton.

Ugh, SCIENCE.

I hear ya.

Where was this taken?

Oh, that's the park by Brace's house.

Y'all hang out a lot, huh?

Yeah, we do! Band stuff just sorta bled into doing whatever after.

Yeah...

That makes sense.

It's gonna be weird going to different schools next year.

Right!

I guess I hadn't thought about that.

JAY, YOUR MOM'S HERE!

THE NEXT WEEK

Map setup?

Yep!

Ms. Fulton went to go find more markers.

M'kay.

Where are you going to high school, Jay?

Weird, Casey was just talking about that.

I guess the IB program at King, where my sister goes. Sounds hard though.

You?

Hopefully Blake, the arts magnet, if they accept my portfolio...

You're not going to apply?

My parents probably won't let me...They're always saying, "You don't want to be a starving artist, do you?"

That sucks.

Yeah...

They still buy me sketchbooks and stuff, so I don't know...

There are a lot of people going to King from our class, at least.

Yeah, Amy and I will probably have the same homeroom. Her brother and my sister do.

Are y'all cool now?

I dunno.

Everything was fine at my party. She even gave me a present. But lately, she barely talks to me.

Hm.

What did she give you?

A purple hoodie.

WHAT?!

What?

JAY.

It's SO obvious she likes you, dude.

But—

Y'know who buys me hoodies?

My mom.

Oh.

Yeah.

That's a nice gift! I don't think I've seen you wear it.

I haven't. It's too hot.

JAY.

There's your answer. I guess you really don't think about people romantically.

A real ace.

Ace?

gulp

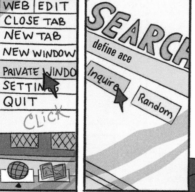

CLICK

- The highest playing card in a suit
- Find local hardware stores in your area

- A person who excels

- May refer to "asexual"

CLICK

- A lack of sexual desire or attraction

- The invisible identity
  - A spectrum
    - Romantic
      - Aromantic
      - Gray-ace

- Some do, some don't
  - Not broken

Hey, whatcha doing?

Solitaire.

You need the computer?

Yeah, if you're finished.

SHUT

Lookit Jay's robot. Just as **fancy** as him!

Thanks, Alisha. I'm not **that** fancy.

Hmm, well you're always dressing up.

Isn't he, Amy?

Yeah, I guess he is... But who cares?

It's just a distraction from his **stupid** face.

HA HA HA

DANG, AMY!

All right, settle down over there.

Sorry, Mr. D.

Jay...

I—I'm really sorry. What I said was mean.

I thought we were friends. I don't understand what I did.

I don't know, you DO always dress up...That's why I got you that hoodie for your birthday.

BOYS

But I guess it's not stylish enough or something since you never wear it.

That's not true!

I love it! It's probably the most thoughtful gift I've ever been given.

Then how come you don't wear it?

Well, I had those rashes on my arms and it's been so hot...

It's always hot! It's Florida! You used to always wear a hoodie.

It's, um...

I've been on this, um...

acne medication, and it really dries out my skin and sometimes makes me feel hot and irritable.

...I can't wear your hoodie right now. I'm sorry.

 Oh.

 Like Accutane?

 YOU KNOW WHAT THAT IS?!

 Yeah, my brother was on it last year. It seemed pretty awful.

It IS awful!

 I can peel **whole** layers of skin off my lips!

Ew, do NOT show me.

 You could've told me, y'know.

It's a weird thing to bring up.

But I really am sorry I didn't wear your gift.

 It's okay. I was holding your book hostage until you did.

 WHAT?!!

That's it.

The last pill.

This kinda looks like the old me...

Jay, breakfast!

Coming!

...but it's still all red.

Is this what I look like now?

We'll be back soon. Need anything?

Where're you going?

My last derm appointment.

The last one. Wow!

Your skin looks great, Jay.

Yeah, I guess so...

I'm curious what Dr. L will say about it.

Jay Violet?

I recommend you get this over-the-counter retinol gel. It'll help encourage skin cell turnover.

All right.

You could use it for the rest of your life if you want, to help your skin stay clear.

I use it myself.

Really?!

It helps with wrinkles, too!

HA HA

Thank you so much, Dr. Laski.

Anytime.

If you have any issues, come back and see me.

I will.

Pencils down, class! Warm-up time is over!

Today, I want us to revisit an old assignment.

Self-portraits! Send a table rep to grab mirrors.

I'll go!

And we'll stick with pencil for now.

Thanks.

REACH

Hey!

What...?

I'm cold.

When I draw my portrait...

...what do I see?

rub
rub
rub

What's wrong, Jay?

It looks **just** like you!

...

You've both improved so much since we began.

Your teacher makes these quizzes pretty challenging.

We'll do lots of review next time.

I'm surprised you missed a few of these, Jay.

The time limit messes with my head sometimes.

But all this extra prep has definitely helped me from second-guessing myself.

Not to worry! Next week, I'll make sure you're **both** ready.

See ya Wednesday, dudes!

Bye! Thanks, Camille.

UGH! No more studying.

SERIOUSLY.

Camille, though. Such a babe.

What about Megan? I thought you were in **love**?

Oh, I am.

And Julie, from last year?

Her too.

Did you and Julie actually date? Or kiss?

Well.

She **did** hold my hand once.

But that was in a dream.

The next day at school, though, she **did** ask to touch my hair!

But I don't think she really liked me.

Casey, how do you know that you like someone?

Hmm.

I don't know...

I just **feel** it.

I want to see them all the time.

I wonder if they're thinking about me.

If they like me, too.

Kinda seems a bit like friendship...

Eh, not exactly.

Friends are different.

I don't want to kiss my friends.

Haha, right.

Are you crushing?! You **never** talk about girls.

Oh, I um...

No, I don't like anyone, I—

Jay, your mom is outside!

See ya at school!

Later J-man.

Ahhh.

Hi.

Hey.

Whatcha drawing?

Nothing really.

The bus is too shaky.

Did you hear? The Rhinos are gonna play at the eighth grade banquet!

That's great.

Jay...

I'm sorry.

We're into different things now...

But you're still my friend.

It's okay.

I know you are.

Do you think, maybe...

...you'd be up for drawing something for the band?

We need an epic backdrop.

Really?

Am I cool enough for that?

Are you kidding? You're the best artist I know!

And guess what?

I got accepted to Blake's music program!

What? No way!

So no IB then?

Nah.

I like music. That's what I want to do.

That's really great, Brace.

I'm happy for you.

So what have you been listening to lately?

Don't say Linkin Park still.

HA HA

HA

Hey! You can take that judgey ska palette elsewhere, mister!

Whoa, whoa, whoa, Jay. Don't EVEN!

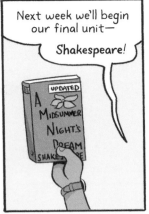
Next week we'll begin our final unit—

Shakespeare!

For our finals, I want to shift away from the incredible solo creative projects I've been seeing and have you work in groups.

GRUMBLE

GRUMBLE

GRUMBLE

Working with others is a life skill. You all have strengths, and an opportunity to learn from others will serve you well as you move into high school.

I'll also be assigning **groups**. Feel free to read ahead and begin your planning.

Pd. 1
Mid Summer
Final Project

Jay
Kristen
Casey

Come ON. We still haven't figured out our project.

I have to pee! Sue me!

This way?

First on the left.

Please don't notice all my skincare stuff in there...

Hellooo? Jay?

Sorry, sorry, I'm listening!

URGH, why did Mr. Harold assign a group project?

It's too hard to agree.

Not to mention meeting across town like this. My dad will be here soon.

Yeah I know. Sorry I live so far out.

There's so little time to prepare, and I want to get an A.

Hear me out, one more time.

NO.

Kristen and I don't play music or sing.

It's not happening, Casey.

Well, I don't want to do some **boring** spoken analysis thing or some tapestry comic, so I guess that's a final curtain on our grade.

WAIT! That's it!

Music, art, **and** performance.

It's practically staring us in the face!

Instead of Titania's monologue, we'll do this part from Act Two. Casey, you'll do the fairy's song to some **guitar-drum thing**, and Jay, you'll design **masks** and **props**. You'll only have to recite **one** line.

What d'ya think?

Works for me.

Me too.

Hope it's a short line.

Excellent. Ours will be the best.

By far!

What're you workin' on?

You've been at that desk for hours.

My English project.

And this thing I'm doing for Brace's band.

I'll need all the cardboard we have!

We have some in the garage. Are you sure you have time for all this? What about your other finals?

I'll be fine.

Plus I won't get to do stuff like this in IB next year.

Lorelai didn't tell you?

She's not continuing there next year.

What? **Really?!**

Where's she going?

Can I apply to Blake?

Blake? It's all the way across town.

And you'll need to focus on more than **art** for college.

I know...

There's a new high school only fifteen minutes away. You won't have to get up at the crack of dawn.

Okay.

And Lore can drive you both.

Me and Dad will finally be **free!**

I might need a new bike helmet then.

Very funny.

Don't stay up too late, hun.

I won't.

ONE WEEK LATER

Mind if I change the channel?

Nah, I'm not even watching it.

What's all this for?

English.

We're doing a short skit from Shakespeare.

You're performing?

I'm trying not to think about it.

Have you thought about us going to the same school again?

Now you can resume ignoring me at home **and** school!

Haha.

The truth is that I probably won't even see you. High school is big.

Yeah.

It'll be weird not knowing anyone. Like sixth grade all over again.

Don't worry. You'll make friends!

I know you're shy, but it'll be new for everyone else there, too. And they'll live nearby.

I guess.

After three years, I feel like I only just found my people.

We're all set up, Kristen!

Perfect. Change quickly and we'll be in before the bell.

Everyone's gonna be looking at me.

I should've asked Kristen to put makeup on us...Stupid stress breakout!!

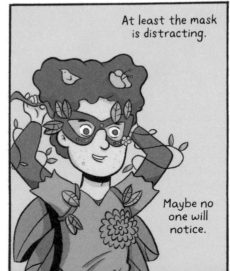

At least the mask is distracting.

Maybe no one will notice.

Guys, are we doing too much? I don't think anyone else is doing this much.

Are you kidding me?

We're getting an A for effort alone.

I hope so!

I'm sweating.

DUDE! You made me into a sick goth fairy!!

Ha Ha

Ha

We all do look pretty great!

This fits perfectly with my dark, lyrical interpretation.

What?! That's not what we practiced!

Worry not, my queen!

GULP

YOU SPOTTED SNAKES WITH DOUBLE TONGUE! THORNY HEDGEHOGS, BE NOT SEEN!

NEWTS AND BLINDWORMS, DO NO WRONG.

COME NOT NEAR OUR FAIRY QUEEN!

PHILOMEL, WITH MELO-DEE, SING IN OUR SWEET LULLABY!

LULLA, LULLA, LULLABY, LULLA, LULLA, LULLABY!

NEVER HARM! NOR SPELL NOR CHARM! COME OUR LOVELY LADY NIGH!

Sorry I ran off.

I got freaked out by everyone looking at me and laughing.

Eh, your line was about leaving, so it worked.

It was pretty funny, too...

And we kinda went for a rock 'n' roll-goth mash-up thing with our costumes, so my music worked too, right?!

I suppose...

Hurry and change. I don't want you to miss the next group.

That was quite memorable and fun... Definitely an A.

Fun...?

Yeah. I guess it was.

Thank you all so much for your help with this.

It means a lot.

No problem. I've never made something that will be seen by so many people.

I'll take this over more self-portraits and landscapes **any day.**

I second you on the landscapes. I wonder what art projects in high school are like?

I hope King has a good art program for us.

Yeah, I think it does...

So we're assembling this afternoon, right?

Yeah, if you still have time.

Yep!

Of course.

Mom's picking me up at four.

ADMIN

Why didn't you tell the truth earlier?

What do you mean?

You're going to that **new** school, Freedom, not King.

I don't know. Like, I already rejected her and now I'm telling her I'm going to a different school?

...It seems mean.

You told her you didn't like her, right?

Well, not exactly...

Tape me!

Perfect.

Hey, Amy, I meant to tell you something.

I'm not going to King next year.

Oh.

Well...that's too bad.

Wonder if we'll end up being football rivals.

Ha! Maybe.

WHOA!

Holy cow, Jay.

Morning.

Morning! You don't need a lunch, right?

Right. Banquet today.

You look so handsome. We **have** to get a photo!

Ugh...Fiiine.

On the fancy chair?

Yes, perfect.

You wanna be fancy, too, Sweetums?

SMILE!

Have a great time. I'll pick you up this afternoon.

Bye, Mom.

One last time.

I'm always catching my reflection these days.

What do I see?

Me.

Jay! Will you sign my yearbook?

If you sign mine, Claire!

It's gonna be weird not seeing you next year.

I know!

Oh my god, we **have** to take a picture!

I'll get Edie.

Okay.

Cute!

It's hard to believe my acne won't return any minute...

DUDE!

What?

The stage!! It looks sick!!

You killed it.

Oh, thank you! I had a lot of help.

But if there's one thing I've learned...

We gotta finish setting up!

Thank the others for us!

Knock 'em dead!

JAY!

Lookin' snazzy.

Thanks, Kristen. You look great, too.

Ooh, spiky hair is **back**.

For a limited time only.

Amy! Alisha! Wow!

...it's that my acne doesn't define me.

It's so fun to see everyone dressed up for once!

Except Jay. Same fancy as always.

I agree!

HA HA

HA HA

HEY!

Author's Note

This book is heavily based on my personal experiences; I think it still feels true, even without being "The Truth."

When it comes to my face, I'm very sensitive. I try not to let perceived vanity keep me from taking care of it, since there is a lot of shame that comes with being concerned over your appearance. In middle school, I was somehow blessed to not be afflicted with acne the way so many of my friends were. But, even as a shy, well-behaved, good student, my peers still found a way to tease me: for my nice handwriting, for gelling my hair, for occasionally wearing a nice shirt, and even for having nice skin by calling me a porcelain doll.

All of my skin troubles began during my senior year of high school, and again at the end of my senior year of college, lasting throughout my mid-twenties. While those may have been less common time periods to experience these ailments, I can assure you that having acne at any age absolutely sucks. Countless ointments, medications, doctor's appointments, and isotretinoin with all its blood work and side effects; I wouldn't wish it on my greatest enemy. All I wanted was to look in the mirror and see myself again. My self-worth and confidence took a major hit during these periods.

At job interviews and places I worked, I thought my acne was perceived as juvenile, and in turn they didn't take me seriously. My inner voice of judgment was hard to suppress when meeting new people, assuming they wouldn't want an acne-afflicted friend. I stopped auditioning for theater and local indie films since I couldn't imagine any director picking me for his leading man with a face like mine. Using clothes as a distraction helped—at least it seemed that way—if someone commented on my outfit, it meant they weren't looking at my bad acne flare-up. But I had flattened myself into one dimension and in my head, acne was my only defining characteristic. I'm immensely grateful to my handful of close friends, who always saw beyond the surface and liked me for myself, acne or not.

Eventually, with the help of a great dermatologist, a second, unpleasant round of isotretinoin, and an enormous amount of patience, my acne troubles did go away. It sounds so simple, but I know it isn't. And what worked for me, won't work for everyone. Even now at thirty-two, I still get breakouts if I don't stay vigilant with my skincare regimen.

This book is also about asexuality, something I wasn't sure I knew how to write about, since it's something I haven't spoken much about in my real life. I didn't even know that word until I was twenty-four, when I heard a character in a TV show use it to casually describe himself. At that moment, something clicked in my head. I immediately opened up a tab on my computer and searched for a definition. I thought I knew what it meant, but I had to verify. And there it was: a clear description of how I'd been my whole life.

Of course, as with any label, these things are fluid, and as time goes on I find that most days it still fits and other days it isn't quite right. But being honest with myself, without anyone else's opinion, is a kind of freedom that I cherish.

I did my best to pull a few threads out of a tapestry to weave a new tapestry, but is it ever possible to say everything in one book? Probably not. Just like one physical attribute or one label can't completely define any one person. And that seems a-okay to me.

Jarad

May 2021

Acknowledgments

Andrew Arnold, for championing me and my story and all of our unexpected life parallels. And for unwavering patience as we made this book during the pandemic.

Kelly Sonnack, for asking me all the right questions and believing in my leap of faith.

Tillie Walden, for encouraging me to be brave.

My family, for letting me sit in my room and draw and for always joking that every incident "is gonna be another chapter in Jarad's book one day." This is for all those times you paged me over the Barnes and Noble intercom. ☺

The amazing team at Harper who all helped *A-Okay* in different ways: Rose Pleuler, Barb Fitzsimmons, Martha Maynard, and Andrew Eliopulos.

My wonderful color flatting assistants: Madi Baker, Sam Bennett, Mercedes Campos-Lopez, Reilly Hadden, Leise Hook, Steve Thueson, and Masha Zhdanova; I couldn't have made this book without all your help. And Shelli Paroline for advice and encouragement when I really needed it.

My friends Katie Cawley, Robyn-Brooke Smith, Steve Thueson, Dan Nott, Daryl Seitchik, Cuyler Hedlund, Ashley Poston, Emma Hunsinger, Natalie Wardlaw, Coco Fox, Chris Crawford, Dave Lloyd, Michelle Ollie, Rachel Tillman, and James Sturm.

And Dr. B for helping me find clarity and teaching me how to take care of my skin.

It takes a village. Thank you all so much!!

For anyone in search of their reflection

HarperAlley is an imprint of HarperCollins Publishers.

Library of Congress Control Number: 2021938242
ISBN 978-0-06-303284-2 (pbk.) — ISBN 978-0-06-303285-9

21 22 23 24 25   EP   10 9 8 7 6 5 4 3 2 1
❖
First Edition